HENRY

JAMES

PERCY

J.P.A

TITLES AVAILABLE IN BUZZ BOOKS

First published 1990 by Buzz Books,
an imprint of the Octopus Publishing Group,
Michelin House, 81 Fulham Road, London SW3 6RB

LONDON MELBOURNE AUCKLAND

Copyright © William Heinemann Ltd 1990

All publishing rights: William Heinemann Ltd. All television
and merchandising rights licensed by William Heinemann Ltd
to Britt Allcroft (Thomas) Ltd exclusively, worldwide.

Photographs © Britt Allcroft (Thomas) Ltd 1985, 1986
Photographs by David Mitton, Kenny McArthur and
Terry Permane for Britt Allcroft's production of
Thomas the Tank Engine and Friends.

ISBN 1 85591 026 8

Printed and bound in the UK by BPCC Paulton Books Ltd.

JAMES AND THE TAR WAGONS

buzz books

Toby is a tram engine. He is short and
sturdy and has a coach called Henrietta.
They enjoy their job on the Island of Sodor.

Every morning they take the workmen to
the quarry and they often meet James at
the junction.

Toby and Henrietta look very
old-fashioned. They were shabby and
needed new paint when they first came,
and James was rude whenever he saw them.

"Ugh! What dirty objects!" he would say as they passed by.

One day Toby lost patience.

"James," he said, "why are you red?"

"I am a splendid engine," replied James, loftily. "I am ready for anything. You never see *my* paint dirty."

"Oh," said Toby, innocently, "that's why you once needed bootlaces – to be ready, I suppose!"

James felt redder than ever and snorted off. It was such an insult to be reminded of the time when a passenger's bootlace had been used to mend a hole in one of his coaches. And all because he had gone too fast.

At the end of the line James left his coaches and got ready for his next train. It was a 'slow goods', stopping at every station to pick up and set down trucks.

James hated slow goods trains.

"Dirty trucks from dirty sidings!" he grumbled.

Starting with only a few, James picked up more and more trucks until he had a long train.

At first, the trucks behaved well but
James bumped them so crossly that they
soon decided to pay him back.

They went over the viaduct and it wasn't long before they reached the top of Gordon's hill. Heavy goods trains should wait there so that the guard can 'pin down' their brakes. This stops the trucks pushing the engines too fast as they go down the hill.

James had had an accident with trucks
once before on Gordon's hill. He should
have remembered this.

"Wait, James, wait!" said his driver, but
James did not wait. He was too busy
thinking about what he would say to Toby
when they next met.

15

"Hurrah! Hurrah!" laughed the trucks. They banged their buffers and pushed James down the hill. The guard tightened his brakes.

"On! On! On!" cried the trucks.

"I've *got* to stop. I've *got* to stop," groaned James.

They thundered through the station and lurched into the yard.

There was a crash and something sticky splashed all over James.

He had run into two tar wagons and was black from smoke-box to cab. He was more dirty than hurt, but the wagons and some trucks were broken to pieces. The breakdown train was in the yard and they soon tidied up the mess.

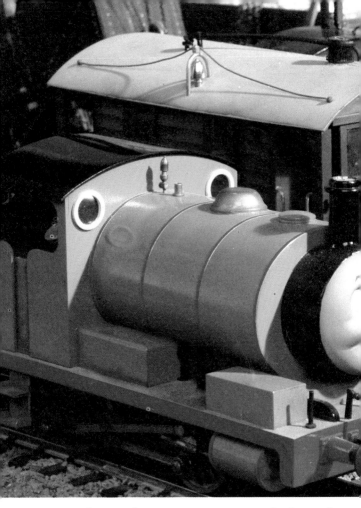

Toby and Percy were sent to help and came as quickly as they could.

"Look there, Percy!" said Toby.

20

"Whatever is that dirty object?"

"That's James," replied Percy. "Didn't you know?"

"Well, it's James's shape," said Toby, "but James is a splendid *red* engine and you never see *his* paint dirty."

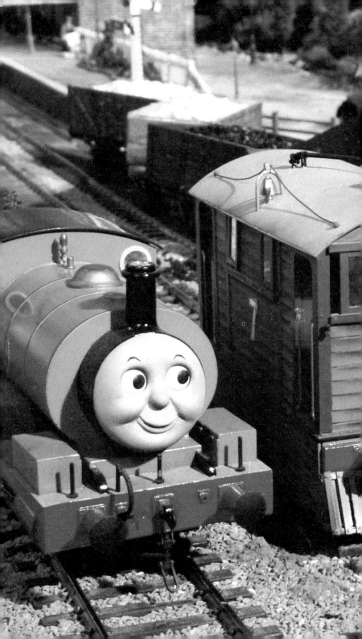

James pretended that he hadn't heard.
Toby and Percy cleared away the unhurt
trucks and helped James home.

The Fat Controller came to meet them.

"Well done, Percy and Toby!" he said, smiling.

He turned to James.

"Fancy letting your trucks run away. I *am* surprised! You're not fit to be seen; you must be cleaned at once," he said.

"Toby shall have a new coat of paint –
chocolate and blue, I think," said the Fat
Controller.

"Please, sir, can Henrietta have one too?"
asked Toby.

"Certainly, Toby," said the Fat Controller. "She shall have brown, like Annie and Clarabel, Thomas's coaches."

Toby smiled. He knew that Henrietta would be delighted and he ran off happily to tell her the good news.

THOMAS

EDWAR

GORDON